THE MYSTERY AT KICKINGBIRD LAKE

GHOST TWINS

THE MYSTERY AT KICKINGBIRD LAKE

Dian Curtis Regan

AN
APPLE
PAPERBACK

SCHOLASTIC INC.
New York Toronto London Auckland Sydney

ISBN 0-590-48253-X

Copyright © 1994 by Dian Curtis Regan.
Map illustration copyright © 1994 by Cindy Knox.
All rights reserved. Published by Scholastic Inc.
APPLE PAPERBACKS is a registered trademark of Scholastic Inc.

12 11 10 9 8 7 6 5 4 3 2 1   4 5 6 7 8 9/9

Printed in the U.S.A.   40

First Scholastic printing, September 1994

*For the Centrum authors
at Ann's annual L.A. sleepover*

Contents

Tuesday,   August 25, 1942   *5 cents*

JUNIPER DAILY NEWS

New Fall Fashions Inside!

Twins Involved in Boating Mishap

Robert Adam Zuffel and his twin sister, Rebeka Allison, seem to be victims of a boating accident at Kickingbird Lake. Their dog, Thatch, disappeared with them. Family members say that the twins had gone hiking on Mystery Island and were probably returning when yesterday's windstorm blew in. Their overturned canoe was floating in the water off Mystery Island. A party of family members searched the lake and the surrounding area, and no trace of the twins or their dog was found.

Today's Highlights

THE MYSTERY AT KICKINGBIRD LAKE

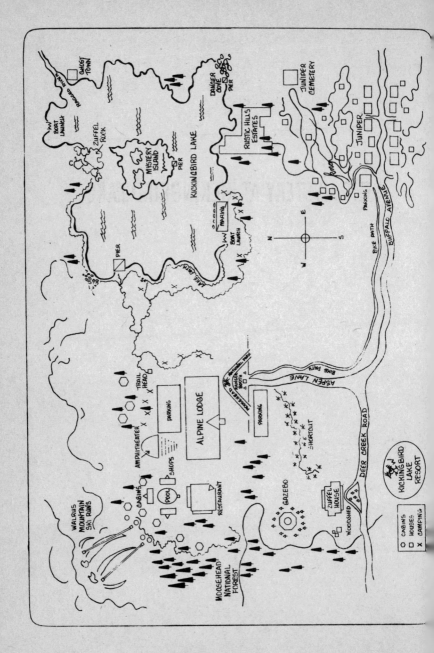

1

Vacation House for Rent

Robbie Zuffel peered out a high attic window overlooking the generous front yard of the "old Zuffel house," as folks had come to call it.

A funny-looking car with luggage strapped on top turned up the drive that curved in front of the wide veranda. The drive's fresh layer of gravel sparkled white in the sun, making Robbie blink.

Was it a car? Or truck? He'd seen similar vehicles drive past the house, but he didn't know what they were called.

Robbie scowled. Being invaded by cleaning crews, painters, and carpenters all month was bad enough. Now they had to put up with people moving in?

"Beka, come here."

Robbie's twin sister glanced up from her place on the braided rug next to the bunk beds. She was finger-combing their dog, Thatch. His unruly white fur with brown patches never stayed in place more than two seconds.

A beam of afternoon sunlight touched Beka's pale face. Sometimes Robbie could see his own face in hers. But more often than not, he couldn't, in spite of all the folks who'd said, "You two look so much alike."

Their hair matched perfectly, though — muddy brown, always caught somewhere in between straight and curly, never making up its mind.

Beka stopped untangling Thatch's fur and hurried to the window. "What's wrong?"

"*That's* what's wrong," Robbie said, pointing.

"I knew it." Beka stepped aside so Thatch could hop onto the window seat and look, too. A low growl bubbled in his throat.

"I knew we wouldn't be here alone forever." She shielded her face from the sunlight. "Well, we did our best to scare off the workers."

Robbie chuckled. They didn't have much practice "haunting" people since they'd kept to themselves the past fifty years. Yet no one had ever invaded their private territory like this before.

The carpenters stayed for weeks, even after finding their nails and tools scattered about the house each morning. The cleaners washed windows, only to find them smeared with fingerprints — and a few paw prints.

The twins liked practicing their "tricks," but nobody noticed. The workers had blamed each other for the pranks. They weren't even scared!

Well, one carpenter was. A girl. She'd said "something weird" was going on around the house, and never came back again.

But the other workers weren't concerned. Robbie thought the *least* they could do was wonder if the girl had been right. Wonder if the old, creaky house *might* be haunted. Ah, well. His ghost pride was hurt.

After the VACATION HOUSE FOR RENT sign went up in the yard, Robbie knew it would only be a matter of time before they'd have to share their home with strangers.

Having the house to themselves had been rather nice all these years. They did what they pleased — played games, read books, stayed up all night, played chase (indoors!) with Thatch. Once, they even had a shouting contest. And no one ever said, "Stop that. Go to bed. Be quiet. Quit running in the house."

3

Robbie and Beka watched the world change, too. The nearby town of Juniper grew from a lunch stop on a country road to a thriving tourist town. Cars and clothes and music changed. Again and again.

The woods in their "backyard" became Moosehead National Park, complete with forest rangers. Homes in the area became vacation rentals as the Tavolott family built their empire: Kickingbird Lake Resort.

Voices below drew Robbie's attention back to the odd vehicle. A girl climbed out, stretching, as though she'd been traveling a long time. She looked about his age — eleven. (Of course, he'd been eleven for fifty years.)

Next came a man and an older boy.

Thatch's ears flew up at the sound of footsteps clunking on the freshly painted steps of the veranda. Before Robbie could say *ghost dog*, Thatch was off, tearing across the attic and down the steps.

The twins laughed. Maybe Thatch would scare the invading family so frightfully, they'd flee from the house and never return.

And if he couldn't, well then, maybe Robbie and Beka — the ghost twins of Kickingbird Lake — could.

2

The Intruders

The twins headed down the attic stairs, around the second floor landing, then down the front steps to the brightly polished hardwood entry hall.

The entire house sparkled with cleanliness. A lemony smell of furniture polish lingered in the air.

Thatch sniffed the intruders, acting as if he didn't know whether to bite them or lick them. Being ignored by all the recent trespassers must have confused his "watchdog mindset."

Sitting on the steps, Robbie felt helpless as he watched their unwanted guests huff and puff, carrying bags and boxes inside.

The girl slumped on a sofa in the family room, her nose in a brochure. Long dark hair tumbled around her shoulders.

"Go upstairs and pick out a room, Kim," the man (her father?) said. "Scott will help carry your bags."

Her brother acted offended. "Can't Miss Shook carry her own bags?"

"Don't start," the man said, sounding tired.

"I knew it!" Kim leaped from the sofa and dashed into the entry hall. "It's right here in the brochure they sent in the mail." She tapped the paper three times to make her point.

Scott leaned over her shoulder to look.

"This is the house." Kim's eyes darted back and forth, taking in the family room and what she could see of the dining area.

"*What* house?" he asked.

"The house no one would buy. For years. Because it's . . . it's *haunted*."

"Oh, right." Scott scrunched his face in exasperation, then hurried up the stairs.

"Our house is *haunted*?" Beka gasped. She imitated Kim, glancing around, wide-eyed.

"They're talking about *us*," Robbie groaned. "*We're* the ghosts."

6

"Oh." Beka gave him a sheepish grin. "Sorry. Sometimes I forget."

The man — Mr. Shook? — ignored his daughter's startling news. "One more trip to the minivan," he said in a dull voice. "That should do it."

"But it's *true*." Kim hollered at him from the doorway. "It says so right here. *'Wispy faces have been seen gazing out the attic windows.'*"

"Wispy faces?" Beka repeated. "*Our* faces?" She gaped at her brother. "Wow, Rob, folks have *seen* us."

"And people have stored things here," Kim added, "then come back to find them moved to a different room."

Robbie raised his right hand. "Guilty, as charged."

They waited while Mr. Shook made one final haul from the *minivan*, as he'd called it. With a stretch and a sigh, he wandered into the family room, sinking into Thatch's overstuffed chair. "Ahhhh. At last, I can enjoy my week's vacation."

Thatch, who'd had enough of watching, lunged toward the stranger who'd laid claim to *his* chair. Rising on his hind legs, the dog tried to climb in, too. But his paws went right through the man.

Robbie winced. The sight always amazed him

7

no matter how many times he saw another person "displacing" their personal space.

Thatch hated being ignored. Dancing around the man, he barked loud enough to startle the nearest neighbor — a good half mile away.

Mr. Shook couldn't hear the barking, of course. Yet *something* made him jump to his feet. "Seems to be a sudden chill in here." Shivering, he folded his arms across his chest.

Robbie hurried to calm Thatch. "It's okay, boy."

Kim entered the room, carrying a pet cage. "Time to free Smudge," she said, setting the cage down and unlatching the door.

A cat zoomed out, then froze, black hair spiking on end.

Robbie gasped at the sight of another pet in Thatch's territory. Especially a *cat*.

Could it *see* the ghost dog? Or merely sense it? The two seemed to be waging a stare-down.

"Smudge, what's *wro* — ?"

Smudge let out a wild *YOWL!* before Kim could finish her question.

In a heartbeat, the cat streaked out of the room and up the stairs — Thatch nipping at her puffed-out tail.

"Gee!" Beka exclaimed. "A cat in Thatch's house! This should keep him entertained."

"Smudge will get used to being here," Mr. Shook said, settling into his chair once more. "Give her a day or two to relax."

"But what if she *saw* them?" Kim's voice was barely a whisper.

Mr. Shook stared at his daughter, looking puzzled. "Saw *who*?"

"The ghosts."

"Kimmie, *forget* ghosts and haunted houses. Go pick out your room and unpack."

"You mean, we're staying here?"

"Of course, we're staying." He imitated her squeaky voice.

She shuddered visibly, tiptoeing toward the stairs. "Well, *I* think we're making a big mistake."

"I think so, too," Robbie said, walking backwards up the steps in front of her.

Beka trailed behind, wearing an ornery grin. "If you truly believe this house is haunted, Kimmie Shook, we'll do our ghostly best not to disappoint you!"

3

The First Haunting

Choosing rooms was easy. Mr. Tavolott's work-ers had decorated the upstairs bedrooms in boy/girl designs.

Scott had already claimed the "boy's room." Posters of baseball teams lined the walls. Navy-blue curtains billowed out at the windows from the afternoon breeze. A matching comforter lay rumpled across the bed.

The clock was shaped like an oversized base-ball. A set of Yankee trading cards bordered the mirror.

Robbie leaned against the bedpost. Seeing fur-niture in his old room again was weird. A few sofas, tables, and chairs had been stored in the house many years ago after it was deeded to the state. (Like the chair in the family room Thatch had claimed.)

But the bedrooms remained empty, which is why he and Beka moved to the attic.

The attic was bright and roomy. High arched rafters gave it a rustic look, along with knotty pine paneling on half-walls. Cutout dormers held window seats, good for curling up in and reading.

(The twins "borrowed" books from the library in Juniper — always making a point to return them within the required two weeks.)

Bunk beds, a dresser with a mirror, and other furniture had been stored in the attic, making it a cozy living area. And, since the windows offered a view in every direction, the twins always knew what was going on in the neighborhood.

Robbie watched Scott unpack and make himself at home. Kicking off his shoes, the boy sprawled across the bed to unload a carton of comic books. *Superman*.

Wow, Superman *is still around*. Robbie had read those back in the forties when he belonged to the Superman of America Fan Club. He remembered the secret code he'd memorized, the special button, and the certificate with his name printed in fancy letters.

Robbie finally gave in to a yawn. Nothing was more boring than watching someone else read comic books. He wandered down the hallway to Beka's old room. Kim was unpacking a suitcase.

Beka waved from the rocking chair. "How do you like my new room?"

The Tavolotts had decorated this one in green and yellow. Old movie posters dotted the walls. Russian nesting dolls perched on a pine desk next to a mini jukebox with a neon bubble tube.

The jukebox really worked. Robbie thought it was nifty. One of the painters kept feeding it pennies, playing what he called "old" songs. But the songs sounded new to Robbie because he'd never heard them before.

Suddenly Thatch padded into the room, head bowed. Had he cornered the cat only to have her zoom right through him? Robbie wondered how Thatch's dog-logic dealt with being a ghost.

Beka stood, wiggling with impatience. "Well? Are you ready to let Kim know she's on the right track? That her vacation house *is* haunted?"

Robbie dropped to the floor next to the rocker. "What do you plan to do?" Their ghost skills were pretty rusty since they hadn't needed them much until the work crews arrived. And simple things like causing nails to scatter and leaving fingerprints on windows had tired them.

That was the problem with being a ghost. Ordinary tasks were much harder. They had to *think* "move" to *make* something move when they touched it. It was a lot of effort for simple actions.

And the only way to renew their strength and energy was to return to Kickingbird Lake. Robbie wasn't sure why.

Beka stepped to the dresser. "Help me, Raz," she said, using the nickname they'd given each other because of their shared initials.

He helped by "thinking" the drawer open as she pulled on it. Finally, the drawer obeyed.

Kim carried two handfuls of socks to the dresser, dumped them into the drawer, and shut it.

Beka opened it again.

The drawer made an eerie scraping sound.

Kim stared at the dreser. "Didn't I just shut that?" Again, she shoved it closed.

Beka opened it.

Kim gasped.

"Yay!" Robbie cheered. "You did it, Bek! You haunted her!"

The girl dropped a stack of shirts, and backed toward the hallway just as Scott came in, holding Smudge. "Hey, Kimmie, let's — "

13

That's all he got out before Smudge sensed Thatch's presence.

Scott did what appeared to be a Mexican hat dance until the cat freed herself from his grasp. With a hair-raising shriek, Smudge was history.

And, with a happy yip, Thatch tore after her.

Scott rubbed his cat scratches. "What's wrong with Smudge?"

"She's being haunted by a ghost dog," Robbie offered.

"More like *taunted* by a ghost dog," Beka added.

"I don't know *what's* gotten into her," Kim whispered. "But forget Smudge and watch this." Gingerly, she closed the dresser drawer once more. "You didn't believe me when I said this house was haunted, so I'm going to prove it to you. Keep your eyes on the drawer."

Beka reached to open it.

"Wait," Robbie said. "Don't do it this time. It'll drive her crazy."

Minutes passed. Nothing happened. "You're wasting my time," Scott grumbled, impatiently running a hand through his hair.

"But . . ." Kim wrinkled her eyebrows, looking confused.

14

Her brother moved to a window and peered at the sky. "Let's hike to Kickingbird Lake before it gets any later. Why waste our first day of vacation staying in the house?"

Kim snatched a sweater from the dresser, acting relieved to be getting out of there. "Is Dad coming with us?"

"Naw. He's on duty. He's making calls on his cellular phone."

"His what?" Beka asked.

Robbie laughed at the goofy face she made. Keeping up with all things modern was difficult. Everything changed fast these days.

"What about Smudge?" Kim asked, following Scott from the room.

"She'll be fine as soon as she calms down."

Robbie stood and stretched. "Having people in our house is costing us energy. We might as well follow them to the lake." He was eager to follow them *anyway* — just for fun.

Although tired, they hurried downstairs. "Thatch!" Robbie called. "Let's go, boy!"

Thatch caught up with the twins as they followed Scott and Kim through the butler's pantry and into the kitchen. Mr. Shook was there, brewing a pot of coffee as he talked on a small phone with no cord.

15

"Look at that!" Robbie exclaimed, stopping to examine the newfangled phone.

He shouldn't have stopped.

Beka and Thatch made it out the kitchen door with Scott and Kim.

But before Robbie could squeeze through, the door slammed shut.

4
How to *Smoosh* in One Easy Lesson

"Crimeny," Robbie mumbled. "I hate closed doors."

Closed doors, locked or unlocked, refused to open for them, no matter how hard they concentrated.

Now there was only one way to get outside. *Smooshing.*

Robbie hated to *smoosh* — mainly because it gave him a throbbing headache.

The twins had discovered *smooshing* by accident. Years after their "mishap" at the lake, they returned to the house. By then it was empty and deserted. The twins stayed in the backyard for

17

weeks, in the gazebo, which nestled in a grove of sugarberry trees.

Every day, Thatch waited by the back door, whining to go inside. The twins wanted to go inside, too, but they didn't know how.

Soon fall weather set in. The nights became colder and colder.

The twins couldn't *feel* the cold, but they could sense the change of seasons. Being inside the house when snow began to fall seemed much better than sitting on wet drifts in the gazebo.

One cold day, Thatch was anything but calm. He kept tearing back and forth across the yard. All of a sudden, he gave a mighty yip, then dashed toward the house and lunged at the kitchen window.

To the twins' shock, the glass didn't break. Thatch zoomed right through a tiny hole in the window — a hole that had been there ever since Robbie played too close to the house with his BB gun.

If Thatch could move through something that tiny, the twins knew they could, too. Making it happen was another story. It took hours and *hours*. Yet it worked. And suddenly they were inside their old, familiar house.

Beka had jokingly called it *smooshing*, and the name stuck.

"Hey!" she hollered from the other side of the window, snapping Robbie back to the present. "Hurry up! They're getting away."

"I know, I know," Robbie muttered.

Thatch put his front paws on the windowsill to gaze in at him, as if the dog was feeling Beka's urgency.

Robbie stared at the hole in the glass. He focused. Concentrated. Willed himself to melt into a mist and zoom right through it. Then come back together on the other side.

A tingly feeling swept over him like a tidal wave.

A million evergreen needles pricked his skin.

A mountain lion roared in his ears.

Robbie opened his eyes. He lay sprawled on the back steps. His head throbbed.

"So glad you could join us," Beka quipped with a smirk.

Robbie shook his head to clear it. "Whew! I'm glad there isn't a screen on that window."

"Why? You'd *smoosh* right through the tiny holes."

"Yeah, but a screen would really strain me."

"Ugh." Beka groaned at his dumb joke. "Come on. I think we're in luck. Scott and Kim don't know about the shortcut, so they went the long way — around the front and down Deer Creek Road."

With that, Beka and Thatch raced across the yard, disappearing behind the sand plum trees that marked the shortcut to Aspen Lane.

Robbie followed, even though he'd rather have sat on the steps and taken an aspirin or two. The headache never lasted long. But while it was there, it hurt more than being bonked on the head with a baseball.

When he got to the road, Scott and Kim were just coming around the bend from the south where Aspen forked into Deer Creek and Buffalo Avenue, the main road that zigzagged through Juniper.

This afternoon, the north route to the lake was crowded with tourists and locals, in cars, on foot, and on bikes.

Robbie kept to the edge of the road. He marveled at the way cars and trucks had changed over the years. No more roadsters and jalopies.

Suddenly his attention was drawn to a crowd of walkers up ahead. A toddler veered away from her family and ran across the road. A park ranger's truck came barreling straight toward her.

Everyone froze.

In a flash, Thatch raced up the road, took a flying leap, and landed on the hood of the truck, barking and yipping like crazy.

The truck skidded to a stop. Inches from the toddler.

The mother ran across the road and snatched up the little girl as the ranger leaped from her truck.

"I — I was distracted," the ranger said in a shaky voice. "I didn't see the child at first. But *something* made me hit the brakes. I don't know what, but I knew I had to stop."

Thatch leaped off the truck, whimpering at the mother's feet, as if making sure the toddler was all right. Then he bounded back to the twins.

"Way to go, boy." Robbie grabbed a handful of Thatch's fur and gave his neck a good rubbing. One thing Thatch had was handfuls of fur. That's how he got his name. His hair looked like the roof of a thatched hut from fairy tales in the twins' old storybooks.

Amazed questions about how the ranger "knew" to hit the brakes skittered through the onlookers. Once they knew the little girl was all right, they moved on up the road.

Beka knelt to fuss over Thatch. "You're always

trying to make up for not saving us that day at the lake, aren't you, puppy?"

The dog nuzzled her cheek, as if agreeing with her words.

"It's okay, Thatch." Robbie took the dog's scraggly face in his hands and gazed into the forlorn eyes circled with brown fur. "It really is okay."

A sloppy lick let him know Thatch was fine.

5

Secret in the Sand

The twins caught up with Scott and Kim. Thatch shadowed them.

Soon they arrived at Alpine Lodge, and the entry arch to Moosehead National Park. They waited while the Shook kids showed a pass to the ranger stationed at a booth collecting park fees.

"Looks like guests of Kickingbird Lake Resort don't have to pay." Robbie steered Thatch through the gate, then waved to the ranger. "We're guests, too!"

Beka laughed, breezing through the gate between two tourists carrying dragon kites to fly.

Robbie felt a burst of energy as he followed Kim and Scott past the parking lot to the hikers' trail that led to the west end of the lake.

Smooshing, in addition to making Kim's dresser drawer open three times, had drained his energy. Being near the lake revived him.

"This place has really changed," Beka said. "Now there's a lodge and restaurants, a swimming pool and shops."

"And tourists," Robbie added.

"Tourists wearing nifty clothes." Beka gestured to her cotton blouse, plaid skirt, and saddle shoes. "I'm tired of these old clothes."

Robbie glanced at his own trousers, shirt, and vest. Clothes he'd been wearing for fifty years. "Me, too."

At the end of the path, Kickingbird Lake spread out almost to the horizon. Sailboats dotted the water like white ducks bobbing up and down.

A group of teenagers sat on boulders along the shore, talking loudly and tossing pebbles into the water.

The air was heavy with the scent of pine and wildflowers. Dragonflies buzzed the surface of the lake. Bees droned. The water rippled in fish rings, as trout rose to the surface to nab a bug for dinner.

Beka sat on a pier to wait while Scott and Kim *oohed* and *ahhed* at the sights. Robbie joined her.

Thatch scampered away to investigate the group of teenagers.

"Cool place," Scott said. "I can't wait to go out in a boat. Dad said something about a lake tour. Maybe we can take it tomorrow."

Kim squinted into the late afternoon sun. "That must be Mystery Island." She pointed toward a jagged chunk of land rising dark and foreboding in the middle of the lake.

"How do you know?" Scott hopped onto the pier to get a better look.

Kim gave an impatient sigh. "Didn't you read any of the brochures? It's called Mystery Island because a lot of strange things have happened over there."

"Like what?"

Robbie followed her gaze, listening to the familiar stories as Kim listed them. He even remembered when some of them happened. Like the bride who jumped off the cliff on the island because her groom didn't show up.

The girl was Rosie Pulaski. The old Pulaski house was south of the lake. The guy she was supposed to marry ran off and joined the army.

Then Kim told a story about some kids whose canoe capsized in turbulent waters off Mystery

Island. How a summer storm came out of nowhere and gave the water a deadly stir. And how no trace of the kids was ever found — except for an empty canoe floating upside down.

Robbie raised an eyebrow at his sister. "Ah, she knows about us. Sort of. *That* might come in handy."

"Let's go exploring." Scott hopped off the pier and cut across the shore away from other hikers.

"Hey," called one of the teenagers. "That path is off-limits." He pointed to a sign tacked onto a cottonwood tree:

PLEASE USE THE PATH THAT CIRCLES
THE LAKE TO THE SOUTH.
THE NORTH PATH IS CLOSED,
DUE TO HEAVY UNDERGROWTH,
UNSURE FOOTING, AND ANIMAL TRAFFIC.

"Thanks," Kim hollered back.

"Why are you stopping?" Scott barreled on through the underbrush. "Going the way everyone else goes is boring. You have to be adventurous."

"But — "

"Kim-mie."

"Well, all right." She stepped gingerly through

the tall grass. "I hope there aren't any snakes hiding in here."

Beka easily caught up with the Shooks. "Didn't we used to hike this way all the time?"

"Yeah." Robbie remembered fishing from the top of the huge boulder up around the bend. It jutted over the water, and was as high as the top of the old Juniper schoolhouse.

"Wonder why they closed the path?" Beka mumbled, holding out her arms to steady herself along the uneven ground.

"Read the sign. Those are three good reasons."

A winding mile later, Kim and Scott stopped at the giant boulder Robbie remembered so well. He'd even named it after himself. Zuffel Rock.

Scott easily found the right toeholds to pull himself to a ledge, then shimmy to the top.

"This is great," Kim said, following his lead.

Beka scurried up the rock. "Come on, Raz. Didn't this used to be one of your old haunts? I mean," she added quickly, "before you became a ghost?"

"Yep." He squinted across the lake. Everything looked the same — even though it'd been a long, long time since he'd been here. His weekly jaunts to the lake to renew his energy usually stopped at the west pier.

Robbie placed his hands against the side of the rock. It felt cold, rough, and gritty beneath his palms.

Remembering each toehold, he pulled himself up the side of the boulder. The top was scooped out smooth in the center, forming a cozy spot to sit, with ample room for a can of worms and a lunch basket.

Thatch remembered the boulder, too. He had his own pathway to the top, starting from the higher ground in back.

Kim settled in while Scott climbed down to the shore to explore the area around the base of the boulder. He called his findings to her: "A school of tadpoles! A broken fishing rod! A dead trout floating on its side!"

The next discovery really captured Scott's attention. He was quiet so long, Robbie almost forgot he was there.

The twins had turned their attention to ways they could let Kim know they were sitting next to her. Could they "haunt" the girl outside the house?

Beka was just about to lay a hand on Kim's shoulder to see, first, if she could do it at all and, second, whether or not Kim would react.

Suddenly Scott shouted.

All three jumped to their feet. Thatch went crazy barking, trying to get off the rock to "save" Scott.

"What is it?" Kim hollered. "Are you hurt?"

"No, it's not that. Get down here. You'll never believe what I found."

Kim took her time stair-stepping down the side of the rock. Robbie took another way he knew was faster. Then he looked up to tell Beka how to get down.

She yanked on the back of his hair.

"Crimeny!" Robbie twirled to face her. "You scared me."

"How can I scare you? You're a ghost."

"Wait a minute," he said, ignoring her comment. "How'd you get down here so fast?"

Beka shrugged. "I jumped."

"You *jumped*? From up there?" Robbie jabbed a thumb toward the clouds. "You could've gotten hurt." As soon as the words were out of his mouth, he realized how silly they sounded.

"Didn't hurt a bit," Beka teased. "You should try it some time."

Robbie laughed at his daredevil sister.

They circled the rock. In the shade of the boulder, Scott was on his knees, hunched over something in the sand. "I found them under there," he said, pointing. "In that dry pocket of sand, sheltered from the weather."

Kim knelt beside him. "Wow," she whispered. "It's like finding a treasure at the end of a rainbow."

Robbie's curiosity was peaked. *What had Scott found?*

Thatch wiggled between the Shooks, sniffing at whatever held the two spellbound. Sometimes Robbie wished his dog could talk.

As he leaned over Scott to look, the boy stuffed his great find into his jacket pocket. Almost as if he *sensed* someone peeking over his shoulder.

"Are you *taking* those things?" Kim seemed shocked.

"Yeah, I'll bet they're worth a *lot*."

"But what if they belong to somebody?"

"Finders keepers."

"What *is* it?" Beka's whisper was impatient.

"I don't know," Robbie told her.

A strong feeling of possessiveness washed over him. This was *his* rock. Zuffel Rock. He'd spent hours and hours here. Even camped out on top of the boulder, sleeping under the stars. He knew every inch of the shore around here. Every cove and stepping stone and fallen branch.

Robbie clenched his jaw. If a rainbow touched down in the sand and left its treasure beneath *his* boulder — then he deserved to know about it.

6
Nice Catch, Thatch

Robbie lay on his bunk bed, watching dawn's first rays paint the attic walls pink.

Ghosts don't sleep. But sometimes they rest, closing their eyes to float among daydreams.

This morning, Robbie's daydreams were *not* pleasant. All he could think about was Scott's big discovery last night at the lake.

Boy, that Kim had quite an imagination. Rainbows don't really touch the earth and leave a treasure behind. (Do they?)

All the way home, the Shooks couldn't stop talking about the "neat stuff." Only they never mentioned the neat stuff by name — which didn't help the twins one bit.

At the house, Scott went straight to his room and closed the door before Robbie could slip through.

"Rats," Robbie had muttered, wondering why closed doors defied his ghost powers. Now he had to wait until morning to steal into Scott's room and go treasure hunting.

Happy dog moans drew Robbie's attention to the east attic windows. Thatch sprawled on his back in a window seat, catching the sun's early rays.

Beka was curled on the floor, holding a book in one hand and rubbing Thatch's tummy with the other.

Thatch loved having his tummy rubbed.

And Beka loved to read. She often took advantage of the first light of day to grab a library book and get started.

"Ready for breakfast?" Robbie called, rising and stretching.

"Very funny," Beka mumbled, keeping her nose in the book. "Ghosts don't eat, remember?"

"Don't *need* to eat, you mean. But we can." He thought about the juicy dill pickles he'd snitched from one of the carpenters' lunches. They'd looked so tempting, he couldn't resist. And the crunchy saltiness tasted better than he'd ever remembered.

Beka peeked over the top of her book. "If I could have breakfast this morning, guess what I'd eat."

"What?" Robbie asked, sauntering to the window.

"Ghost toast."

"Cute," he said, rolling his eyes. "I'd have . . . a bowl of ghost toasties."

"Good one," Beka said. "And ol' Thatch here could have a bone from a ghost roast."

"Where are you getting these terrible jokes?" Robbie glanced at the cover of Beka's book. A typical Halloween ghost wearing a white sheet grinned back at him.

"*Ghost Jokes,*" he read out loud. "By Skel A. Ton. Ha! *We* could have written this book."

"Only if we were ghost writers," she quipped, imitating the cover phantom's grin.

The smell of coffee floated past Robbie's nose. The Shooks were out of bed. Hearing voices below seemed strange after years of quiet in this old house.

Thatch scuttled to his feet at the first noise. Racing across the attic, he disappeared down the steps.

Beka stood, pulling up her socks. "Well? Are

you ready to uncover the *secret treasure* of Kickingbird Lake?"

"You bet. Let's hope Scott has opened his bedroom door by now."

The twins visited the kitchen first, to make sure
Thatch was all right.

The Shook family circled the table, eating
breakfast.

Thatch sat on his hind legs, begging for a bite.

"It's no use, boy," Robbie told him. "They don't
even know you're here. Come upstairs with us."

No amount of urging could get Thatch to leave
the kitchen.

"Watch it," Scott grumbled as Kim bumped his
arm, tipping a plate of bacon. Two pieces slipped
to the floor.

Thatch moved so fast, he caught one piece in
his mouth before it landed. The other, he scarfed
down in less time than it took Scott to lean under
the table.

"Hey, where'd it go?" Hanging upside down,
Scott's gaze circled the floor.

"It fell under Kim's chair." Mr. Shook turned a
page of the morning newspaper. "Get a napkin to
wipe up the grease."

Robbie tugged Beka's sleeve. "Let's watch and
see what happens."

Thatch rolled onto his side, happily licking his snout.

Robbie was amazed that Thatch's ghost powers worked much easier than theirs. Or did they? Wasn't Thatch totally focused on the bacon? The same way he and Beka focused on the dresser drawer to make it move? *Hmm.*

Scott's head stayed under the table a long time. Finally, he slipped from his chair, dropping to his hands and knees to look. "It's *gone*," he said.

Mr. Shook folded the *Juniper Daily News.* "Save your practical jokes for outside, Son. The Tavolotts spent a lot of money fixing up this kitchen. Tile looks brand new. Don't want to ruin it."

Scott thumped Kim on the leg. "Help me."

She dove under the table.

"Do you see any bacon down here?" he asked.

Kim squinted at the floor, swooping her hands under each chair. "Nope."

Robbie and Beka couldn't keep from laughing.

"Ki-ids," Mr. Shook muttered. "Quit teasing your old dad."

"We're not." Kim peeked over the tabletop. "The bacon really *is* gone. It just disappeared."

The man joined his kids under the table.

Robbie was laughing so hard, he had to sit down.

Mr. Shook circled the floor on his hands and knees. "Well, this is the strangest thing I've ever seen."

"*Not* seen is more like it," Beka said.

One by one, the family returned to their places and resumed eating. No one spoke. They were trying to figure out what had just happened.

Kim put down her fork and sat stone still. Her face looked as white as the milk in the jug. "May I be excused?" she finally asked.

Mr. Shook nodded.

Pushing away from the table, she ran from the room, glancing behind like someone was following.

But no one followed. Not yet. Robbie and Beka stayed to see what conclusion the other two would make about the missing meat.

"Son, did I see two pieces of bacon fall to the floor?"

"Yes, sir."

"But now they're gone."

"Right."

Mr. Shook picked up another strip of bacon.

Robbie knew in an instant what the man planned to do. Thinking fast, he grabbed Thatch's collar and led him into the butler's pantry, out of sight.

"What's happening?" he called to Beka.

"Two people are staring at a piece of bacon on the floor," she said, giggling. Then, "You can come back now. They picked it up."

Robbie let Thatch go, and stepped into the kitchen. Thatch instantly found the spot where the bacon had fallen, licking it clean.

"Guess I haven't had enough coffee this morning." Mr. Shook poured another cup. "I'm imagining things."

Scott, his nose in the comics section of the newspaper, had already forgotten the episode.

"Show's over." Robbie took hold of the dog's collar again. "Let's get up to Scott's room before he finishes eating. If Thatch can pull practical ghost jokes, maybe we can, too."

"What are you thinking?" Beka raised her eyebrows a couple of times.

"I'm thinking about making something *else* disappear. Like the mysterious treasure from the rainbow's end."

7

Brain Drain

Whatever secret Kickingbird Lake had whispered to Scott, it refused to repeat to the twins.

They combed every inch of the boy's room. Nothing they found seemed unusual — or interesting enough to match the Shooks' reaction.

Thatch was in the middle of everything — as usual — "helping" with the search.

Robbie poked through a few more nooks and crannies. "I don't get it," he said, slumping on the bed. "Where did Scott hide his great discovery?" The effort of opening drawers and cupboards was beginning to tire him.

Beka climbed on top of a chair to take one last look on a high shelf. "Maybe the items are still in Scott's pocket."

"I looked."

Beka cocked her head. "You searched his pockets?"

"Yeah. In the trousers he wore last night." Robbie motioned toward a pile of dirty clothes in one corner.

"Oh, right. He's wearing shorts today."

Suddenly Scott burst into the room, flopping onto the bed before Robbie had time to react.

Rolling out of the boy's way, Robbie came to his feet on the other side of the bed. But not before half of Scott's body sliced through his.

"I hate it when that happens," he muttered, leaning against the window frame as far from Scott as he could get.

The brief interaction made Scott shiver, rubbing his bare arms. "It's chilly in here all of a sudden. I'd better take a sweatshirt." He lifted a pair of clunky-looking boots from under the bed and pulled them on.

"They're going out," Beka said. "Great. Now we get the whole house to ourselves."

Robbie watched Scott grab a hooded top. (A *sweatshirt*?) He shoved it into a pack like the one

Robbie used to carry school books in. "Let's follow them, Bek."

"Why? I thought you wanted to get rid of the Shooks. They're leaving for the day. Let them go."

Robbie gingerly sat on the corner of the bed, careful not to get in Scott's way. "Yeah, but . . ."

"But what?"

"Don't you think having people around is nifty? And listening in on conversations is fun?"

Beka didn't respond.

"I don't *want* to get rid of them now," Robbie told her. "I mean, weren't you getting bored, hanging around an empty house all the time?"

She gave a weak shrug. "I like hanging around an empty house."

"Where's my baseball cap?" Scott muttered, sticking his head inside the closet.

"Right there." Beka pointed toward a hook. While Scott's back was turned, she took hold of the cap. After a few moments, it moved in her hand. Whisking the cap off the hook, she tossed it onto the bed.

It shimmered. Then sparked a blue flash.

The twins figured out long ago that when they "claimed" something, it became invisible to people. When they let go, the shimmering and sparking meant it was becoming visible again. To the human eye.

"It's not in here." Scott backed out of the closet. His gaze traveled the room, landing on the cap. "Hey, how did — ?"

"Ready?" Kim appeared in the doorway. She carried a pack like Scott's, strapped to her back.

"Almost. Meet you downstairs."

Scott shoved the baseball cap into the pack, then paused, as if trying to make a decision. Pulling out a dresser drawer, he rummaged through the clothes, becoming more and more agitated as he searched.

"Kimmie!"

His sister returned. "You told me to wait downstairs."

"You *took* them."

"Them?" Robbie echoed.

Kim shifted from one foot to the other, not answering.

"You aren't allowed in my room," Scott snapped. "At home *or* here. First, you moved my baseball cap, then — "

"I didn't touch your cap."

"It wasn't where I put it." Scott moved to shut the bedroom door, lowering his voice, as if he didn't want his father to hear them arguing.

"Give them back to me. They're not yours."

Kim hooked her thumbs around the straps on the pack. "They're not yours, either."

"Why'd you take those things from me?" His voice cracked.

"Because you can't sell them. It's not right."

"Do you have a better idea?"

"Yeah. We should return the things to their rightful owners."

Scott shot her an impatient look, as if she'd just suggested spending the day on Mars. "How?"

"I'm going to the newspaper office in Juniper this afternoon to place an ad. Whoever lost those things can come by and claim them."

"We'll see." Scott smirked, like he knew something she didn't. "Come on. Let's go play tourist," he said in a grumpy voice as they left.

"So, Kimmie stole her brother's secret." Beka slid to the floor to rest.

Robbie was tired, too. Even Thatch sprawled on top of Scott's desk. "I hope the Shooks head to the lake first. I'm suffering brain drain. A shot of energy would greatly help."

"We can't follow them *now*, Rob." Even Beka's voice sounded weak. "I'll bet Kim hid the stuff in her room. Let's search there while she's gone."

"You're right." Robbie hesitated, torn between wanting to discover Scott's secret — and tagging along with the guy just for fun. His mind gave in to the *fun* part. "Bek, I *really* want to *go play tourist* with the Shooks."

"You're whining," she said. Then, "Okay, go. *I'm* the one who wants the house to myself. I'll stay here and search Kim's room."

"But if your energy is drained, you need — "

"I'm fine." She pulled herself to her feet, yet she seemed to be moving slower than normal.

"Look." Beka pointed out the window. "Kim has discovered our shortcut already. Go, Raz, or you'll lose them."

"Okay." Robbie clicked his fingers, rousing the dog. "Thatch needs to get out and run anyway."

But instead of heading down the stairs, Robbie went out the open window. He climbed onto the landing overlooking the backyard. "Want to go for a walk, Thatch?"

Walk was a people-word Thatch understood. In one smooth leap, he was outside.

"What are you doing?" Beka asked, leaning out the window. "Thatch can't climb down the tree."

Robbie ducked under a thick branch of the blackjack oak. His sister's leap from Zuffel Rock had given him a daring idea. "We don't *have* to climb down the tree."

With that, he leaped from the roof, landing softly on the deck below.

"Copycat!" Beka called, teasing him.

Thatch paced back and forth on the ledge, whimpering.

"Come on, boy," Robbie urged.

Finally, the dog jumped, landing as smoothly as his master.

Beka waved as they ran across the yard. "Have fun playing tourist," she called. "And while you're away, I, Rebeka Allison Zuffel, will personally solve the mystery of Kickingbird Lake."

8

Legends of the Lake

Robbie followed the Shooks through the short-cut to Aspen Lane. Yes, they were going to the lake. He was glad. If they'd headed toward town, he couldn't have followed far without running out of steam.

The closer he got to the lake, the better he felt. As his energy returned, he picked up a stick for Thatch to chase — after making sure no one was watching.

Thatch loved chasing sticks. And he *usually* brought them back so Robbie could toss them again.

One wild throw almost clipped Kim. "Whoops!" Robbie yelped, then, "Sorry, Kimmie!"

He half expected her to yell back. "That's okay, Robbie."

But she didn't. Instead, she twirled, as if she'd heard the stick whiz past her ear. Heard it plop into rustling leaves.

Kim stared at the spot as Thatch snatched up the stick and raced back to Robbie.

Had she seen the stick "appear" in the leaves? Then disappear again when Thatch grabbed it?

Robbie was never sure what people saw.

Arriving at the ranger booth near Alpine Lodge, Kim and Scott bought tickets for the lake tour. The tour was a new attraction, added this summer by Mr. Tavolott. The twins had planned to take it someday as invisible stowaways.

"One, please," Robbie told Ranger Parella. "And a pet pass for my dog."

Of course she didn't see him.

When they got to the lake, the tour boat was docked at the pier. Robbie and Thatch stepped up a plank, swept along with the crowd.

Teenage workers, called junior rangers, helped people board, answered questions, and served snacks from large trays.

They directed Scott and Kim (and Robbie and Thatch) to the upper deck for the best view.

"Welcome aboard," boomed a voice over a loudspeaker. "I'm Ranger Diaz, and I will be your guide."

The boat chugged away from the pier, and sailed past the marina, where canoes could be rented for trips to Mystery Island. Also for rent were boats with big paddles in the back. Passengers moved the paddles by pedaling, as if they were riding a bicycle.

Robbie thought the boats were nifty. He remembered the dinky canoe he and Beka had been in the day their boat capsized. Maybe if they'd been in a bigger canoe, or one of the paddle boats, the accident would never have happened.

As the tour boat picked up speed, the breeze grew brisk. Passengers pulled on sweaters and zipped up jackets. Scott took the baseball cap and sweatshirt from his pack. Kim untied a sweater from around her waist and put it on.

Robbie kept one hand on Thatch's collar to hold him close. He never knew what kind of mischief a ghost dog might get into.

As the boat circled Mystery Island, Robbie daydreamed, half-listening to Ranger Diaz tell the familiar stories native to the area.

The sudden mention of his own name over the loudspeaker instantly drew his attention. Robbie stared at the ranger through a window in the captain's bridge.

" . . . and his twin sister, Rebeka," the ranger was saying into a microphone. "They lived in the old Zuffel house on Deer Creek Road. Kickingbird Lake wasn't part of a national park in those days, but served as a playground for all who lived in the area."

Murmurs echoed through the crowd as people commented on the story.

"The twins must have known the lake as well as they knew their own backyard," Ranger Diaz continued. "But one day, they misjudged it. Storms blow in quickly here, turning ripples into choppy waves. Sometimes our tour boats stay docked when the lake gets too rough."

Robbie's face burned in embarrassment as he listened to the ranger's words. He and Beka and Thatch had joined the other legends of the lake!

"No one knows what happened that summer day," Ranger Diaz said. "But the twins' canoe capsized, dumping them and their dog into the water."

"The Zuffel house!" Kim blurted, making Robbie jump. "Scott, I *knew* that sounded familiar. That's the house we're staying in."

"So?"

"So, the brochure mentioned ghosts. But it didn't go into detail. It didn't say the ghosts were *kids*."

Scott shushed her because the ranger was still talking.

"And a dog," she whispered. "Two kids and a dog."

"You read too many scary books," he whispered back. "You're starting to believe everything you read."

"I'll prove it to you." Kim raised her hand as though she were at school.

"I believe we have a question," Ranger Diaz said, nodding at her.

"Sir," Kim began, "the house you mentioned, the one the twins lived in, is that the house that's supposed to be haunted?"

Everyone within hearing distance laughed.

Kim didn't like being laughed at. She set her jaw and frowned at the surrounding crowd. "Well, is it?" she demanded.

Ranger Diaz stalled for a moment, as if trying to think of a good answer. "Let me just say that the owners of Kickingbird Lake Resort don't squelch the rumors. They enjoy keeping legends alive in hopes that they're good for business."

More laughter.

Kim twirled around and gazed across the lake.

The wind whipped her hair *through* Robbie's face. He stepped back.

"Don't ask dumb questions," Scott hissed at her. "You embarrass me." He worked his way across the deck as far from his sister as he could get.

Under her breath Kim mumbled. "If the ghost kids are in our house, I'm going to find them."

Robbie chuckled. "Hear that, Thatch? She's going to *find* us. Shall we make it easy for her?"

When he reached to touch Thatch, his hand met empty air.

The dog was gone.

Robbie pivoted, trying to spot Thatch wandering among the passengers. He'd absently let go of the dog's collar, and was too intent on the ranger's words to notice Thatch had disappeared.

"I'll be back," he said to Kim, then made his way *through* the crowd to the steps.

On the lower deck he came to an abrupt stop. A robust lady in a flowery dress and hat was perched on a bench showing pictures to a companion. In her lap was a plate piled high with snacks from a junior ranger's tray.

Thatch, his nose in the lady's lap, was busily gobbling the treats off her plate.

9
Missing Snacks and Floating Freckles

"**T**hatch!" Robbie shouted. "Get over here."

The dog turned one eye to look at his master, then ignored the command and continued licking the plate.

The lady, still talking to her companion, reached to lift a treat from her lap. Stopping, she gasped at the empty plate.

Robbie didn't like the way the lady's hand and Thatch's head were taking up the same space. In two steps, he grasped the dog by the collar and yanked him away.

The lady turned to a man sitting next to her, quietly peering at the scenery through binoculars. "The nerve!" she exclaimed in a shrill voice.

Startled, the man leaped to his feet. "I beg your pardon?"

"*Hmmph*," was all she replied, so the man hurried away.

Robbie groaned. He kept a firm grip on Thatch for the rest of the tour.

At noon, back on land, Scott and Kim parted ways.

Robbie was torn. Scott planned to take a series of hiking trails that wove through the foothills of Walrus Mountain. (The peak resembled the head of a walrus. Twin ski runs cut through the pines like long tusks.)

Kim headed toward the town of Juniper. Robbie figured she was going ahead with her plan to put a lost-and-found ad in the newspaper.

Since he couldn't decide which Shook to follow, Robbie went back to the house. Besides, he was eager to find out if Beka had located Scott's treasure somewhere in Kim's room.

At home, he toured the downstairs, then the second floor, looking in all Beka's favorite spots. She was nowhere to be found.

Next he tried the attic. They usually avoided it on muggy summer afternoons because the heavy air seemed to slow their thoughts and movements.

Beka wasn't on her bunk or in any of the window seats.

"That's odd," Robbie mumbled.

He returned to the family room where he'd left Thatch, curled in his chair for an afternoon nap. (Robbie was never sure if the dog actually slept, or just *floated*, the way he and Beka did.)

"Thatch, wake up." Robbie pulled him from the chair. "Find Beka."

Thatch's ears flew up, as if he felt Robbie's concern.

Sniffing the air, Thatch *woofed* a few times, then headed toward the kitchen. The back door was propped open to cool the house. Mr. Shook was in a lounge chair on the new cedar deck, built last week by the workers.

Robbie and Thatch rushed outside. The tangy scent of fresh cedar still flavored the air.

Thatch tore across the yard.

The gazebo! Of course! Beka liked to read there.

In the middle of the gazebo, a swing hung from two chains below the pointed roof. Robbie found his sister stretched out on the swing. He sat on the built-in bench circling the inside of the octagon-shaped structure.

Thatch sniffle-snorted around his mistress, trying to rouse her.

She didn't move.

"Beka? Are you all right?" Alarm surged through Robbie. She looked pale and wispy. He could see the swing right through her!

Quickly he moved to shake her shoulder. "Sis, what's wrong?"

Beka turned to gaze at him. Her freckles seemed to float in midair, looking for a solid face to land on.

"Hi," was all she said.

"What happened?"

"Searched Kim's room. Didn't find anything. Looked through entire house. Got *really* tired, but I promised you . . . I promised. . . ."

Getting words out was too much effort, so she stopped.

"You need a doctor," Robbie blurted, before he realized the silliness of his words.

Beka gave a faint laugh. "Like who? Doctor Spook?"

"Cute." Robbie frowned, still concerned. "We have to get you to the lake. You've drained too much of your energy."

Thatch took hold of Beka's shirt and tried to tug her off the swing.

Robbie helped his sister stand, but her legs were wobbly. "Remember when we used to give each other piggyback rides?"

She put her arms around his shoulders. He hoisted her onto his back, looping his arms under her legs. Off the trio went through the shortcut, the quickest route to Kickingbird Lake.

Halfway there, Beka felt strong enough to walk. Robbie watched her. She seemed less hazy now, but her freckles still looked dark against her pale face. One by one they stopped floating as they found a solid face to land on.

The twins went all the way to the lake, just to make sure Beka was all right. Sitting in the sun on the pier, she looked quite normal.

"I scared myself," she told him. "I *smooshed* through a knothole in the woodshed, and couldn't get out." She rubbed her head, remembering. "I finally did, obviously, but it took a lot of effort. Guess we'd better be careful not to drain all our energy."

She nudged her brother's shoulder. "Thanks for taking care of me."

"You'd have done the same for me."

Robbie filled her in on Ranger Diaz and the tour boat ride while Thatch chased butterflies in a patch of orange wildflowers. Then Robbie brought her up to date on Scott and Kim. "It's too late now to interfere with Kim going to the newspaper."

"She must have taken the stuff with her," Beka said. "I'm *positive* it isn't in the house."

The annoying delay in finding Scott's treasure only added to Robbie's curiosity about it. He doubled his determination. The mystery would be solved. By him. Today.

Now overflowing with energy, the twins raced Thatch to the house.

Thatch won, of course. He always won their races.

10

The Secret Treasure
Revealed

The twins arrived at the house to find the Shook kids already home from their afternoon jaunts.

Scott was tossing a tennis ball against the house, then catching it in a mitt. Kim was trying to skate on the wooden deck.

"Look at her skates," Beka said, gaping at them. "They're like ice skates, but with a row of wheels instead of blades."

Frustrated by skating in too small an area, Kim plopped onto the steps to take off the skates. "Why'd we stay somewhere with no sidewalks or paved streets for Rollerblading?" she grumbled.

"Kids!" Mr. Shook hollered from the door. "I want to talk to you."

Scott (and Thatch) chased a grounder. Inches from the dog's jaws, Scott swooped it smoothly into the mitt.

"Lucky move," Robbie mumbled.

"Into the house," Mr. Shook ordered. "Both of you. Now."

Four kids and a dog scrambled into the kitchen.

"Sit."

They all sat around the kitchen table.

Thatch began to whine.

Robbie followed the dog's gaze. On top of the refrigerator, Smudge hunched like a vulture, glaring down at them. Well, mostly in Thatch's direction.

Robbie wondered if the cat's name had anything to do with the uneven "smudge" of black fur across her white nose. It looked like she'd been nibbling on a gooey chocolate bar.

Mr. Shook placed a rolled-up towel on the table. It was white, with KICKINGBIRD LAKE RESORT stamped in fancy letters at one end.

Kim gasped at the sight of the towel.

Scott heaved a sigh and glared at his sister.

"I found this hidden in my sock drawer," their

father said. "Would somebody care to tell me what it is and why it was there?"

"You hid them in his *sock drawer?*" Scott snarled.

Kim placed a protective hand on the towel, like it would prevent Scott from dashing off with the precious contents. "I was running out of places to hide them."

"Who do these belong to?" Mr. Shook asked, sitting at the table.

Scott leaned back and crossed his arms, as though he planned to let Kim do all the talking and take the blame.

"We don't know," she said. "But tomorrow's newspaper will carry a lost-and-found ad. If no one claims these, then I guess . . . I guess we can keep them?" Her statement turned into a question aimed at her dad.

He shook his head. "They look valuable. And I don't think you can count on the owner seeing your ad if it runs only one day."

"It's all I could afford." Kim obviously hadn't expected her noble gesture to be criticized. "Ask Scott what *he* planned to do with them."

Her attempt to get her brother into trouble didn't work, so she added, "*He* planned to *sell* them."

Mr. Shook was too busy unfolding the bundle to respond.

The twins leaned forward in anticipation as the towel fell away, exposing Scott's *secret treasure*.

The sight took Robbie by surprise.

Beka caught her breath. "Rob!" she hissed. "It's your gold watch! The one you inherited from Grandfather. And my silver locket. And look! Thatch's old chain collar with his name on it!"

Amazed, Robbie could only whisper, "It's all the things we had with us that day at the lake."

"Hey, you cleaned the dirt and grime off." Scott looked impressed. "And polished them, too."

"When I went into Juniper, I took them to a jeweler," Kim explained with modesty. "That's why I only had enough money to place the ad for one day." She frowned at her dad until he noticed and patted her arm.

For a moment, no one spoke. Passing the items around the table, they examined them one by one.

"*Thatch*," Scott read, studying the tag on the dog collar.

Thatch's ears flew up at the mention of his name. For an instant, he was distracted from his staring contest with the refrigerator cat.

"What a dumb name for a dog," Scott added.

"Hey, watch it." Beka swiped her hand at him,

but it went right through his shoulder.

"*R.A.Z.*," Kim said, reading the initials on the watch. "*Hmmm.*" She raised an eyebrow. "What did Ranger Diaz call that boy?"

"What boy?" her brother asked.

"The boy who misjudged the lake that day? The one whose boat capsized?"

Robbie felt insulted. *The boy who misjudged the lake?* What a thing to be remembered for.

Scott slipped the watch onto his wrist. "How should I know his name?"

"Wasn't it Ricky? Or Randy?"

"Don't remember."

"I want my locket back," Beka said, inches from Kim's face. "*Now.*"

Robbie understood how his sister felt. Sitting here looking at *his* watch on *Scott's* wrist was a lesson in patience. "Are you going to — ?"

Before he could get the question out, Beka thrust her hand forward, grabbing for the locket.

Robbie tensed for the scream he knew would come when the locket suddenly disappeared.

But Beka's hand dipped right through Kim's, locket and all.

"Rats," Beka muttered. "We can't claim our things as long as people are touching them."

"Well." Mr. Shook finished his inspection. He

made Scott remove the watch, then rolled the twins' possessions back in the towel. "I'll call the newspaper and extend the ad for a week. If no one claims these before we go home, we'll leave them at the ranger station in Alpine Lodge."

"Awww, Dad," Scott groaned.

"Your sister is right. They don't belong to us."

He set the bundle on top of the refrigerator. Smudge immediately sniffed it, then sprawled across the towel.

"*Now* we can get them." Beka climbed onto the counter.

"Shouldn't we wait until the Shooks leave?" Robbie wasn't so sure about making things disappear in front of a kitchen full of people.

Beka hesitated. "I won't do it while they're watching."

She didn't have long to wait. Scott flew out the back door. Mr. Shook wandered into another room. Kim was the only one who stayed — keeping her eyes on the bundle with a cat on top.

"Shall I try to distract Kim so she'll glance away?" Robbie asked.

"Why bother? She's seen us move things before."

"Oh, that's right, her dresser drawer."

Beka stood on tiptoes and grabbed for the

towel. But her hand went through it, thanks to the cat. "I forgot," she mumbled. "As long as Smudge is there, I can't take hold of our things."

"And with Thatch down here," Robbie added, "the cat's not going anywhere." He sighed. "Give it up, Sis. We'll come back later when Smudge is gone and claim *what's rightfully ours*, as Kim would say."

Now Robbie knew what the big secret was. And why it bothered him so much. It *did* have something to do with them. Pieces of their lives. *Getting our possessions back will feel good*, he told himself.

Beka hopped off the counter. As she passed the table, she shouted into Kim's ear, "Robbie! The boy's name was Robbie! And in case you forgot, he had a sister — Rebeka. That's me!"

Robbie's laugh caught in his throat as Kim jumped to her feet, knocking over a kitchen chair. "Robbie!" Kim blurted, as if she'd received Beka's message, loud and clear. "The boy's name was *Robbie*!"

11
Footsteps in the Attic

Robbie planned to sit on the deck and watch the cat through the kitchen window, waiting for the moment she jumped off the refrigerator.

But rain began to fall.

He didn't like rain. Not because he got wet — he didn't. He disliked watching raindrops zing through his body as though it wasn't there.

The sight was a spooky one.

After convincing Thatch to give up his job of guarding the cat's escape route, the twins left him happily snoozing in his overstuffed chair in the family room. Then they wandered to the attic.

Beka had claimed the top bunk fifty years ago, so that's where she settled. Robbie lay down on the lower bunk to rest. The sound of falling rain amid the rumble of distant thunder soothed him, lulling him into a trance.

His mind drifted back to the tour of Kickingbird Lake. How had he and Beka become one of the resort's "tourist attractions"?

He thought about the day they'd returned as ghosts. He had suddenly "awakened" on the far shore of the lake — in the water. He'd waited for Beka, who waded toward shore as if she had all the time in the world.

He remembered the cold wind that kicked up, and how he didn't feel cold *or* wet. Not even chilled. He remembered Thatch bounding down the shore, so happy to see him, like he'd been gone for years.

The twins couldn't figure out why they weren't wet, even though they'd been in the water. Then they couldn't figure out why they were even *at* the lake in the middle of the night. That's when Robbie checked the time, and found his watch gone. Lost somewhere in Kickingbird Lake.

On the hike home, they ran into Mr. Nelson, out in his milk truck, leaving bottles of milk in boxes on people's front porches.

"Wow, it must really be late if the milkman's

out," Beka said. *"Early*, I mean. Maybe he'll give us a ride home."

"Mr. Nelson!" Robbie yelled.

Mr. Nelson didn't answer.

Robbie ran up to him. "Sir, can you take us home? We've lost track of the time, and — "

Mr. Nelson acted as if Robbie wasn't even there.

"Sir?" he said again. "Can't you hear me?"

The man had hoisted two bottles of milk by wire handles, and walked up the path toward a house. Walked right through Beka.

That's when they figured it all out.

That's when they knew they were ghosts.

Robbie shifted on the bunk bed, floating on to other daydreams.

He wasn't sure how long he "napped." Footsteps in the attic made his eyes pop open.

In the darkness of the afternoon rainstorm, a figure appeared, tiptoeing quietly toward the bunk beds.

Robbie shot up straight, first confused, then scared. Seconds later, he realized the intruder was Kim — clutching the rolled-up towel. What was she doing?

Something in her face and mannerisms reminded Robbie of Lucy Moreno, a girl who'd tormented him all through third grade. She'd teased him about his last name, saying things like, *"Zuffel rhymes with Zoo-full, which means you belong in a zoo."*

Before Robbie could get out of the way, Kim plopped onto the bed.

"Gee!" he cried, scrambling to his feet. She'd sat down right on top of him.

Leaning against the ladder at the foot of the bunk beds, he waited to see what she planned to do.

"I have to find a good spot to hide these things," Kim mumbled to herself. "Dad won't like it, but if I don't put them in a safe place, Scott will take them. I just know he will."

Pausing, she unwrapped the towel to take another look.

Robbie leaned over her shoulder. He knew he couldn't pick up his gold watch while she held it, but he wanted to see it again. So many years had passed since he'd looked at it.

Suddenly, Kim stuffed the watch back into the towel to hide it from view. She shifted sideways, almost as if she'd heard someone sneaking up behind her.

The girl frowned into the dim light. Frowned right through Robbie.

Robbie grinned. Could he scare her? Like Beka did yesterday? Kim looked so much like Lucy Moreno, Robbie *wanted* to haunt her.

"Raz, help me out." He stepped up the ladder to rouse his sister.

Beka was reading. Thatch was stretched out next to her. He must have missed them when he woke up alone downstairs.

"*You* can do it," Beka said, hanging upside down from the top bunk to watch. "You don't need my help."

"You mean, you want me to haunt her all by myself?"

She grinned. "Be my ghost."

Robbie hopped off the ladder. Kim was now underneath the bunk, searching for a good hiding place. She stood, dusting herself off.

"Here goes," Robbie said.

Beka nodded her approval.

"*Eww-WEEE-ewww!*" he singsonged.

His sister laughed. "What's *that* supposed to mean?"

"It's ghost talk." Robbie danced around the bunk, waving his arms and singing, "*Mares eat oats, and does eat oats, and little lambs eat ivy.*"

Barking, Thatch leaped from the upper bunk to see what was causing all the commotion.

Kim stood like a statue against the dresser, her mouth gaping open.

Robbie felt stupid. Beka was better at this sort of thing. An attack of self-consciousness made him stop his song and dance.

Kim kept staring in his direction.

For a minute, Robbie thought she could actually see him. Either that, or his singing was way off key.

He thought of the *ghost rumor* about "wispy faces at the attic windows." Maybe the attic was the only place they were visible, since that's where they spent most of their time.

"Kimmie?" he whispered, just in case.

"I — Is somebody there?" Her voice was barely a whisper.

In the dresser mirror, she appeared to be staring off into empty space. Maybe she merely *sensed* the presence of another being.

"I'm Robert Zuffel," he said, offering his hand. "Nice to — "

Kim dove under the bed, swooped up the bundle, and was down the attic stairs before Robbie could finish saying "meet you."

"I did it," he laughed. "I haunted someone." He

finished his dance without feeling self-conscious. "And I think she saw me."

"She didn't see you." Beka climbed down the ladder. "She said, *'Is somebody there?'* She didn't say, *'Who are you?'* "

"Right."

Beka frowned at him.

"What's wrong?"

"Oh, Rob, if only you'd left her alone, she wouldn't have taken back our things. She'd have left them under the bunk — which means we'd have them right now."

"Crimeny." Robbie sank to the bed. He hadn't thought of that. "Sorry, Bek. Guess that wasn't too brilliant of me."

"Come on." She pulled him back to his feet. "Let's tail her. The minute she sets the bundle down, then — *POOF!* — it's ours."

"*POOF!*" Robbie repeated. "I like the sound of that word. Has a ring of magic to it — ghost magic."

12

The Sugarberry Library

Downstairs, Scott slouched in front of a boxy screen that flashed moving pictures. The box had been delivered last week with other pieces of new and used furniture. Robbie and Beka didn't know what it was.

"Look!" Robbie pointed at the screen. "It's like a tiny movie theater, right here in the house."

Beka sank to her knees in front of the quickly moving images.

"Where's Dad?" Kim asked, not even glancing at the box.

How could Kim ignore this wonderful invention? Robbie was amazed.

"He went fishing. I didn't want to go." Scott

flipped something in his hand, and the image on the screen changed.

"Did you see that?" Beka's eyes were wide. "He made the story change when he moved his hand."

"We're supposed to get a pizza for dinner," Scott said. "Dad left money on the table."

"I'm not hungry," Kim told him. "I'm going into Juniper."

He glanced at his sister. "You're going into town by yourself? Why?"

"I need to go to the library, and, um, look up some information."

Robbie knew exactly what information Kim was looking for. Information about that *boy who misjudged the lake*. And who now, rumor said, haunted the old Zuffel house.

"Want to come with me?" Kim asked, pulling on a white rain jacket with a hood.

"Naw, the game is on next. Just be careful."

"Be careful?" Robbie repeated.

"Yeah, there might be ghosts around," Beka reminded him, not taking her eyes from the screen.

"Oh, ghosts. I forgot." Robbie wished he could stay and watch the game, too — whatever game it was. Monopoly, maybe? "Come on, Bek. Kim's leaving."

"Wait a minute."

On the screen, a police car sped wildly after a zigzagging truck.

Robbie didn't want to wait. He'd already lost a chance to get their possessions away from Kim. He didn't want to mess up again. The moving picture box would be here when they got back.

The kitchen door slammed. "Oh, great. Kim left already. Now what?"

He knew what. *Smooshing*. He touched his head in anticipation of another rip-roaring headache.

Grabbing his sister's arm, Robbie yanked her to her feet.

"But, I want to know who the lady in the truck is and why the police are chasing her," Beka complained.

"We've got more important things to do right now." Robbie hurried into the kitchen, calling Thatch. The dog came bounding in after him.

"Here, boy." Stooping, Robbie wrapped both arms around the dog, then focused on the BB-sized hole in the window. "Outside, boy," he whispered in the dog's floppy ear. "Think *outside*."

Beka *smooshed* first. A gust of wind hit Robbie in the face. When he looked, his sister was gone. Seconds later, she waved at him through the window, leaning against the deck railing to recover.

"*Think*, Thatch," Robbie whispered, feeling the dog's muscles tense. "*Think*, Zuffel," he muttered to himself, focusing on the hole in the window.

Dizziness swept over him. Pins pricked his skin. The lion roared in his ears. He and Thatch tumbled onto the deck.

Robbie crawled to a step to sit, dropping his head into his hands. Thatch sprawled flat on the deck. Did dogs get *smooshing* headaches, too?

Beka started across the yard. "Come on, gang. Kim's getting away!"

Thatch scrambled to his feet and tore after her.

"Why does it take me longer than anyone else to recover from *smooshing*?" Robbie pulled himself up and trudged after them. His pounding head wouldn't allow him to run.

Rain still fell from a charcoal sky. All in all, it seemed a good evening to stay inside and read — or watch moving pictures. Robbie thought about "borrowing" a few of Scott's *Superman* comics to read tonight in the attic.

Catching up with Kim was easy. Not because they could move faster, but because they didn't get winded or tired when they hiked.

Robbie suspected they could walk for hours — except for one problem. The further they hiked from the lake, the lower their energy level. It hadn't taken them long to discover that leaving the resort area was impossible.

After the shortcut, Kim turned south, veering east when the road forked. They followed her down a path that ran alongside Buffalo Avenue all the way to town.

The path was for bikes, Robbie had noticed one day, and for people who liked to run. A lot of grown-ups ran up and down the roads these days for no apparent reason. Robbie thought it was strange.

The rain let up, leaving a nippy chill in the late afternoon air. The few passersby who'd ventured out were bundled in jackets and long pants. The sky threatened to cut loose again, so most of them carried umbrellas.

Soon the bike path gave way to the sidewalks of downtown Juniper.

The cozy town seemed inviting to Robbie, the way it nestled in a valley between two hills. Today, dark clouds drifted below the hilltops, leaving the town under an eerie gray shadow.

Once, Juniper consisted of shops, homes, and gas stations along a short section of Buffalo Avenue. Now the town stretched for miles, with buildings rising halfway up the hills on both sides.

Many of the homes were patterned after Swiss chalets. Bright colors and stenciled flowers decorated houses. Window boxes overflowed with late summer flowers.

Businesses sported homey names: Aunt Emma's Muffin Shoppe, Grandma's Engine Repair, and the Sugarberry Library — which Robbie thought was fun to say.

Kim hurried up the steep stone steps of the library and pushed through the double oak doors. The twins and Thatch stayed right on her heels — making it through the doors before they slammed shut.

As many times as Robbie had been inside the library, he'd never gone there for information about himself. The anticipation of reading "the story of Robert Zuffel" thrilled him and chilled him at the same time.

13

What Really Happened

At the information desk, Kim asked a bearded man for help. His name tag said STAN in purple letters. Robbie had seen him before in the library.

His skin was so pale, the twins once decided he'd spent the entire summer behind library walls. (Or maybe he was a ghost, too — ha!)

Kim asked Stan how to find an old story in the newspaper. Stan thought by "old" she meant "last week." He seemed surprised when she asked for papers from the 1940s.

Quickly, she filled him in on the story she was looking for.

"Ah," Stan said. "The Zuffel twins." He paused

to think, absently stroking his beard. "My grand-mother used to talk about the twins. Let's see. The accident happened about ten years before I was born." ·

He led Kim to a microfilm viewer and asked her to wait. Then he disappeared into a back room.

Robbie and Beka settled on each side of Kim. Thatch wandered off.

"Shouldn't we keep Thatch here?" Beka asked.

Robbie shrugged. "How much trouble can a ghost dog get into in a library?"

Beka agreed.

Stan returned with several rolls of microfilm. He turned the viewer on, and showed Kim how to thread the film into the machine.

"I've narrowed it down to several years," Stan said. "Finding the exact day should be easier because it happened late in August. Most of the mishaps on the lake happen when summer's mild weather gives way to fall's storms without much notice. Many folks have misjudged the lake."

"Misjudged the lake," Robbie muttered. *There's that phrase again.*

Stan left. Kim began to scan the film.

"Wrong year," Beka said, leaning back and acting bored.

They waited until Kim gave up and tried the next film.

"Good, you've got the right year," Beka told her. "Keep going, keep going. The day you're looking for is August twenty-fifth — the day after the *mishap*, as everyone calls it."

Finally, Kim spotted the feature. All three leaned forward to read the story.

"*Ewww*, what an awful picture," Beka groaned. "I always hated that dress with the pink daisy pattern. And I'm not too fond of *this* skirt, either." She paused to brush off imaginary lint. "I mean, I've worn it for fifty years."

Robbie laughed. He thought he looked rather handsome in his hat and vest. After studying the picture, he turned his attention to the story.

Kim read in silence. "Wow," she finally whispered. "I wonder what *really* happened that day."

"Well, you see," Beka began. "Rob and I were waiting by the marina for our cousins to arrive."

"We'd planned to take a canoe across the lake to Mystery Island, and go on a picnic," Robbie added. "Our cousins never showed up, so we went by ourselves."

"Even though it was too late in the day to stay on the island very long," Beka said.

"We took the smallest canoe," Robbie continued, "thinking it'd be easier to row. Thatch kept rocking the boat. I practically had to sit on him to make him stay still."

"We docked at the pier on Mystery Island, and hiked up a path we'd never taken before," Beka said. "It was fun."

"Yeah," Robbie agreed. "But we stayed too long. By the time we started back, the sky had turned almost black. The waves lifted the canoe like it was a toothpick, then sent us on a roller-coaster ride."

"Over and over and over." Beka folded her arms across her stomach, as if remembering how sick it had made her. "I got scared. We should have spent the night on the island. But we were afraid we'd be in big trouble if we didn't get home on time."

Kim found another version of the story in the next day's paper. Focusing the words with a turn of a knob, she continued reading while the twins told her *what really happened.*

"The ride was so rocky," Beka said, "I knew I was going to be sick. So I leaned over the side."

"You leaned too far," Robbie told her. "Thatch jumped up to see what was wrong with you. He tipped the canoe."

"I fell into the lake."

"We both fell in. Then Thatch landed on top of me and pushed me under." Robbie paused. The blurred images seemed long ago and far away, like scenes from a silent movie.

"I remember . . ." he began. "I remember being cold. I hit my head on something — a rock or the canoe. After that, I don't remember anything at all."

Kim finished reading the story, leaning back in her chair to think — or to listen to their version of the account.

"I don't remember my brother being in the water at all," Beka told her. "I just remember Thatch tugging on my shirt. I grabbed his chain collar — the one you have in your pocket right now — then my foot tangled in something. That's all *I* remember."

Kim clicked off the viewer.

Robbie wondered if any of their silent words had woven their way between the lines in the newspaper story.

"It's hard to believe," Kim whispered to the dark screen. "But the dog's name *was* Thatch, which means this *is* his old collar." She placed a hand on top of her pocket. "The watch must belong to the boy, Robbie. His initials were R.A.Z. And the locket must belong to his sister, Rebeka."

Kim stood abruptly. "The twins *are* haunting their old house. And they want their things back. We've upset them." She hugged herself. "Will they hurt us?"

Kim shivered in spite of the fact she wore a heavy sweater under her rain jacket. "There's only one thing to do," she mumbled. "Give Scott's treasure back to the ghosts. But how?"

She paused, thinking, then snapped her fingers to seal her decision. "Of course. It's simple. All I have to do is return the twins' possessions to Kickingbird Lake."

14
A Ghostly Plan

Kim hurried through the library, waving good-bye to Stan.

The twins stayed close behind so they could make it through the doors when Kim went out.

"Wait," Beka put on the brakes by the checkout counter.

"What now?" Robbie felt frustrated by his sister's chronic delays.

"We're forgetting something."

· As soon as the words were out of her mouth, a shriek echoed through the bookshelves somewhere upstairs in the quiet library.

Shrieking wasn't allowed in a library. It could only mean one thing.

"Thatch!" Robbie hissed, dashing for the stairs. *"That's* what we forgot."

The steps quickly crowded as library patrons rushed to find the source of the screaming. Two security police joined the fray.

On the second floor, a young man knelt by an older woman, stretched out on the floor. He attempted to revive her by fanning an issue of *National Geographic* across her face.

Nearby sat Thatch, looking innocent. His head was cocked to one side as he watched the scene with interest.

Robbie worked his way through the people and grabbed the dog's collar — the rope collar they'd made after his chain collar was lost to the lake.

He led Thatch to the steps.

"Hold up," Beka said. "Let's find out what happened."

One of the security police began to question the man.

"My mother was browsing through the romance novels," he said. "Then she sat at a table to look at the books. I was across the way in Periodicals, but I noticed she'd taken candy from her purse."

He paused. "My mother has a . . . *uh* . . . *condition,* so she carries snacks with her."

He threw a guilty glance toward the officer, as

if he hoped his mother wouldn't be arrested for bringing food into the library.

The policeman jotted notes on a tablet, then nodded for the man to continue.

"All of a sudden, Mother screamed. I rushed to her. Before she fainted, she told me that . . . uh . . . an invisible person — or *thing* — licked her fingers after she ate the candy."

Robbie groaned as Beka giggled.

The man glanced at the surrounding crowd, as comments echoed around him. "It's true," he said. "Ask Mother when she awakens."

"The man *is* telling the truth!" Robbie called to the spectators. "My dog can hear a candy wrapper being unpeeled a mile away."

With that, the twins headed downstairs. They waited patiently by the front doors until the next person came in. Then out they went, heading up the street after Kim.

As they hurried along, Robbie wondered how Thatch had broken the barrier and made contact with a person. The dog seemed able to do things they couldn't. He'd been the first to *smoosh*, and now the first to actually touch someone. Were Thatch's powers greater than theirs? *Hmmm.*

They were almost home before they caught up with Kim.

Scott was still hunched in front of the movie screen. A baseball game was on.

"Ah," Robbie said. "*That* kind of game. Now I get it."

"Scott, I have to talk to you," Kim huffed, tearing off her jacket.

"Wait till the commercial," he said.

"No. It's important." She glanced around. "Is Dad still fishing?"

"Yeah, I told you he wouldn't be back for dinner."

Kim punched a button on the moving-picture box. The sound quieted, but the picture remained.

"What'd you do that for?" Scott raised his hand, aiming something toward the screen.

Kim stepped in front of the box.

"Move," he said.

"I figured it all out," she told him, unable to conceal her excitement.

"You figured *what* out?"

"I know who the ghosts are."

"The ghosts? You mean, you're still on that ghost kick?"

"That ghost kick?" Beka repeated.

Scott sighed. "Turn off the TV."

"TV," Robbie repeated. "That's what they call it."

Kim punched a button and the screen went dark.

"So, talk," her brother said.

"The ghosts haunting this house are the *twins*."

"What twins?"

"The ones in the boating accident on the lake."

"You mean, the accident that happened years and years ago?"

"Yep. Plus, I have reason to believe that the stuff you found at the lake belongs to the ghosts. And they want their possessions back."

"Okay, Sherlock, how do you know all this?"

"Well, first — the deal with my dresser."

"What about your dresser?"

"The drawer kept opening on its own."

"So you say."

"Then there's Smudge. She hasn't acted normal since we arrived."

"Cat's don't travel well. I can't believe Dad let you bring her. She would've been better off staying with one of your friends." Scott shook his head, as if he thought his sister was digging for nonsense clues. "What else, Kimmie? I want to get back to the game."

"The *real* reason Smudge isn't acting normal is because a dog is after her. A *ghost* dog."

"Ha!" was all Scott said.

"Then how do you explain the missing bacon?"

"You mean, you think a ghost dog lapped the bacon off the floor?"

"Yes. What do *you* think happened to it?"

Scott didn't have an answer for that one.

"Then there was the thing in the attic."

"What thing?"

"Yeah, what thing?" Robbie echoed.

"I felt like something was watching me. I . . . I could feel its presence. And when I looked, I saw this hazy image. At first I thought it was sunlight coming through the window, but it rained all afternoon, remember?"

He didn't answer, so she continued. "Then the haze sort of swirled into a figure. I think it was a boy."

"She thinks you're a boy," Beka teased. "But she's not sure."

Robbie gave her . . . *a look*.

"Then he — the boy — held out one hand, like he was asking me for his watch."

Scott seemed terribly amused. "So where was his twin? And the dog?"

"I — I don't know. I didn't see them."

"Kimmie, I think you've been out in the rain too long. Your brain is soggy." He reached for the instrument that controlled the movie screen.

Kim stopped him. "The *point* is that the ghosts want their stuff back, so I'm taking it to the lake. Right now. Will you go with me?"

Her words yanked Scott from his chair. "You took it off the refrigerator?"

She nodded. "I left the towel there so Dad wouldn't notice, but the twins' things are right here." She patted her pocket.

"Are you crazy? Dad's gonna find out, and he's *not* going to like it."

"He'll be pleased to know I returned the treasure to its proper place."

Scott's face turned red in frustration. "What if the owners answer your ad in the newspaper?"

"They can't."

"Why not?"

"Because the owners are *ghosts*. Get it?"

Giving up, he paced to the window. "You can't go to the lake now. It'll be dark soon. And it looks like another storm is rolling in over the hills."

"Well, *I* don't want to spend a stormy night in a house with angry ghosts. Do you? Come on, Scott. Let's go appease them."

She pulled on her jacket.

"I'm not going," he said. "Neither should you. What am I supposed to tell Dad when he gets home and you're not here? *I'll* be in trouble."

"You're not my baby-sitter. And besides, all you have to tell Dad is the truth." Kim flipped around and hurried toward the kitchen.

"Hustle," Robbie said. "So we can make it through the door."

This time, Beka didn't argue.

As they hurried across the back lawn, distant thunder shook the earth like a bad omen.

Beka peered at the gloomy sky. "Hey!" she hollered to Kim. "Listen to your big brother. This isn't a good night to go out."

"Besides," Robbie called, "there's an easier way. Just hand over our stuff right here and now. Then we can all go inside and watch the baseball game, safe and dry."

But Kim barreled on through the shortcut.

Then Thatch did something unusual. Instead of sticking with the twins, he raced ahead, catching up with Kim, running alongside her — almost as if he knew she needed protecting tonight.

The sight of his dog shadowing Kim so closely made Robbie nervous. He only hoped Thatch's dog-hunch was way off base.

15

POOF! It's Ours

Every step closer to Kickingbird Lake, the temperature dropped another degree. Or so it seemed.

The breeze turned into a serious wind, whipping leaves from the trees before they were ready to fall, and kicking sand into faces along the road.

Traffic moved in only one direction — away from the lake. Tourists seemed anxious to get home to their vacation rentals before the angry-looking clouds let loose with another downpour.

Robbie thought the feel of wind gusting *through* him was an odd sensation. Strange that none of the rules of the world applied to them.

He also thought Kim was crazy for thinking she

had to go to the lake on such an unpleasant evening. No way could she get there and back before darkness settled across the hills.

If only she would take the items from her pocket, set them down, *and* remove her hand, then he and Beka could claim their possessions.

They'd be happy. Kim would be happy.

Yet, it *didn't* mean they'd quit haunting her. Robbie rather *liked* the haunting business.

When they arrived at Alpine Lodge, no one was in the booth collecting park fees. A sign had been taped in the window:

KICKINGBIRD LAKE RECREATION AREA
IS CLOSED TONIGHT
DUE TO POOR WEATHER

"Good," Beka said. "Kim will have to wait until morning."

But Kim merely hopped the gate and headed toward the hikers' path.

"Hey," Beka called. "Didn't you read the sign?"

"Guess not," Robbie said.

They had no choice but to follow.

As Robbie hiked the path, strength and energy surged through him from the lake. Feeling terrific in such miserable weather seemed strange when it sent everyone else scurrying for shelter.

Beka was doing a hop-step along the path. Robbie assumed it meant she felt good, too. Thatch was chasing ahead, then dashing back to Kim, as if he overflowed with excess energy as well.

The mile hike to Zuffel Rock was slow-going. Kim pulled up the hood on her rain jacket with a gloved hand to shield her face from windblown debris. Walking into the brisk gusts seemed difficult to her.

At one point she mumbled, "They'd better appreciate this."

Robbie felt badly about her suffering all this agony for nothing.

At the giant boulder, Kim stopped, as if listening for ghost voices riding on the wind. Gingerly, she stepped around the rock to the shore where the "rainbow" had ended, leaving its treasure.

The rock served as a good windbreak, allowing Kim to pull off her hood and gloves. Reaching into her pocket, she removed the items one by one, then held them straight out in front of her.

Closing her eyes, she began to mumble.

"What's she doing?" Beka whispered.

"Looks like she's performing a ceremony before she returns our stuff," Robbie said. "To appease our anger, as she told Scott."

"We're not angry."

"I know that, but *she* doesn't know that." Robbie watched for a moment. "Gee, I hope she doesn't pitch our things out into the water. We'd *never* get them back."

Thatch hunched nearby, waiting, as if he knew a solemn ceremony was taking place.

With a sharp crack of thunder, the sky opened as it'd promised, dumping torrents of rain on the group, and bringing a quick end to the ceremony.

Kim knelt next to the rock, placing the items in the sheltered pocket of sand where Scott had found them. It seemed like forever before she stood and backed away.

Beka waited for Kim to disappear around the boulder. "Now!" she yelped, diving toward the hidden spot.

Grinning, she removed the *treasure*. "*POOF!*" she cried. "It's ours."

Beka examined her locket, then held it out to Robbie. Turning, she lifted the back of her hair.

Robbie put the chain around her neck, fumbling with the clasp a few times before he hooked it.

Then he lifted his watch from Beka's hand. It was ticking! Silently, he thanked Kim for taking it to a jeweler.

He slipped it around his wrist, then grabbed

Thatch's old collar. "Here, boy!" Robbie glanced around. "Where'd he go?"

Beka stopped fiddling with her locket. "He must have headed back with Kim. Good. Thatch will make sure she gets home safely."

No sooner had Beka said the words, then Thatch began to bark.

Above the howling wind, a shrill scream split the air, followed by a faint *splash*.

The sound filled Robbie with horror.

He'd heard it before.

It was the sound of a person falling into the lake.

16

More Secrets in
Kickingbird Lake

The twins bolted down the path to find Kim. Thatch's wild barking stopped them.

They looked up. In the dimming twilight, they could see the dog peering at them from the top of the boulder.

"Did Kim climb up *there*?" Beka had to shout the question because the wind was making so much noise. "In the rain?"

"She must have." Robbie was torn. What should they do? If Kim was injured, every second counted. And if she was in the water . . .

His mind didn't want to finish the thought. "Climb the rock and try to spot her," he hollered. "I'll look from down here."

Beka scrambled up the boulder, using the toe-holds. "Wow, it's slick and slippery from the rain," she yelled. "How'd Kim ever make it up here?"

Robbie worked his way around the edge of the rock formation. Thatch's barking sounded a definite alarm, but it didn't help. Didn't tell Robbie what to do.

He hopped onto a row of stepping stones, venturing out a few yards into the lake, scanning the surface of the water.

Night was falling fast, thanks to the thick blanket of clouds. If they didn't find Kim within the next twenty minutes, twilight would give way to total darkness, making it impossible. Then what?

Whitecapped waves splashed right through his legs. Sometimes being a ghost had its advantages — like stepping into the wild waves of a freezing lake without getting cold and wet.

"Bek! Can you see anything?"

"I found Kim's bracelet up here!" Beka yelled back. "It's broken. She must have slipped on the wet rock and fallen. Robbie you've got to find her!"

Thatch went crazy, racing back and forth on the rock cliff. Finally he leaped. His white fur helped Robbie track the dog's dive.

He waited, hoping Thatch would dog-paddle to Kim, pointing the way.

Precious seconds slipped by. Thatch had simply disappeared. "I'm going in!" Robbie shouted to Beka. He started to add, "Run for help!" but that wouldn't work. How could she tell anyone Kim was in danger?

"Be careful!" his sister yelled back.

Seemed like a dumb thing to say, but Robbie would have said the same thing to her.

"Rob!" she screamed. "Somebody's coming! With a flashlight!"

He caught her message an instant before he dove.

Robbie swam toward the spot where Thatch had disappeared. The dog was nowhere in sight. *How could that be?*

Diving under, Robbie kicked hard, then pulled himself along the underside of the boulder. The giant rock jutted out over the water, but did not go all the way to the bottom of the lake.

Halfway around, he decided to duck under the rock. Two feet inside, the rock curved up. Robbie broke the surface. A cave! The rock formed an underground cave!

Although pitch-black inside, Robbie could make out the image of a white dog and a white jacket — which had to be Kim.

Making his way toward them, his feet touched

bottom as the ground sloped toward shore. He found Kim lying in shallow water, her head on the sand. She was breathing. Robbie sighed with relief.

Thatch hunched beside her, whining. He knew she was in trouble.

Robbie patted his fur, marveling at how it could still be dry underneath a lake. "Good job, Thatch. She's okay." He squinted into the blackness of the rock prison enclosing them. "The question is — How do we get her out of here?"

Robbie knew his hands would go right through Kim's arm if he tried to lift her, but he tried anyway. He was right. "It's no use," he mumbled. "I can't save her."

He thought about the episode at the library and how Thatch had made contact with the lady's hand. Maybe the dog could drag Kim out of the cave.

Using his hands to "see," Robbie picked up Thatch's paw and placed it on Kim's arm. The paw fell through to the sand.

"So much for that idea. What *else* can we do?" Quickly he felt his way around the cave, wishing he'd known about it fifty years ago. Exploring it — or turning it into a clubhouse — would have been great fun.

Thanks to waves rolling constantly to shore, the area seemed to be a final resting ground for lots of things lost in the lake. He found a beach ball, various articles of clothing (he guessed by touch), fishing poles, a life preserver off someone's sailboat, and . . .

"A life preserver!" Robbie stopped searching. He could touch it. Now all he had to do was concentrate hard enough to make it move. He couldn't touch Kim, but if he could get the donut-shaped ring around her, he could pull *that* out of the cave and she'd come with it.

"Brilliant, Zuffel," he mumbled to himself. Then he put both hands on the life preserver, and concentrated harder than he ever had before.

Along the edges of his mind danced his name. Someone was calling him. Beka. She was probably frantic, wondering what happened to him. And Thatch. And Kim.

Beka's panic kept filtering into his mind, breaking his concentration. Mentally, he shoved her away. She'd understand, once she learned what was going on.

A minute must have passed before the life preserver moved in his hand. Finally! Now he had power over it.

Quickly he waded back to Kim. Putting the ring

over her head, he forced it into the mushy sand she lay on as he tried to pull it around her. But the tube stopped at her shoulders.

Yanking it off, he guessed where her feet must be, then slipped the tube around her legs, pulling it up through the soft sand until it fit under her arms.

Thatch tried to help, but there wasn't much he could do.

Robbie turned Kim by dragging the tube around until he could catch hold of it with one hand on each side, under her arms. That way he could keep the tube in place.

With a final sigh, he backed into the deep water. When the ground gave way, Robbie kicked hard.

"Come, Thatch!" he hollered before his head went under. Robbie knew he had to be quick. There was no way he could tell Kim to take a deep breath before dragging her under water.

Her weight slowed him. A mixture of urgency and panic made him kick harder. Forcing the life preserver down into the water until they cleared the rock took all his strength. Life preservers weren't made to stay under.

Faster, faster! his mind screamed as he kicked. Kim was swallowing water now, but there was nothing he could do about it.

Finally his hand felt the boulder curving up. Robbie braced a leg against the rock and shoved away. As they zoomed through the water, he kicked like crazy until they broke the surface.

White light blinded him for a second. Someone on top of the rock was swooping a flashlight across the waves. Swiftly, the light returned, playing on Kim.

"Kimmie!" a voice shouted.

Was it Scott?

Robbie stayed with her, making sure her head remained above water. He kicked toward shore to make it easier on her rescuer.

The light wiggled erratically, as if someone was scaling down the boulder as fast as they could. Then the light stopped. Moments later, Robbie heard someone splashing toward them in the water.

He let go of the life preserver. It shimmered, sparking red.

An arm wrapped around Kim. "Are you okay?" The panic-filled voice was Scott's.

"She is now," Robbie said.

He and Thatch dog-paddled until their feet hit bottom.

Beka met them on shore. "Quick thinking," she said, giving him an okay punch on the shoulder.

Thatch gave a good shaking. Robbie figured his dog-logic told him he was wet when he wasn't.

The twins watched Scott struggle to get Kim ashore. He placed her in the sand and pulled off the life preserver. Kim was coughing and choking. Scott pounded her on the back until she started gulping for air.

"How'd you get Scott to look for Kim in the right place?" Robbie asked.

"I borrowed your ghost talk. I planted myself in front of him and yelled *'Eww-WEEE-ewww!'* until he stopped and decided to climb the boulder."

"I had a bad feeling about you coming out here alone," Scott said, sounding out of breath. "You're lucky I followed you."

Kim moaned an answer.

"What were you doing on top of the rock?"

The wind snatched her answer and threw it away. Scott didn't catch any of it, but Robbie did. Kim had climbed the boulder to wait for the ghosts to come collect their things. She'd wanted to see them.

Scott helped her stand, but her legs wobbled. He groaned as loudly as the wind was howling. "You mean, I have to carry you all the way home?"

"Wait." Kim dropped to her knees, stretching to reach into the secret place under the boulder.

"They're gone," she said, gasping as if the words weren't coming easily. "The ghost twins came and took them."

"What?" Scott covered one ear to block the wind.

Kim didn't answer.

He handed the flashlight to his sister, then hoisted her into his arms. "You weigh a ton," he grumbled.

In the glow of the flashlight, Kim wore a satisfied smile. "Let's go home," she said.

"Great idea," Robbie agreed. "How about you, Thatch? You worked the hardest of all tonight."

"Woof!" was all Thatch said.

17
Who Rescued Whom?

"Now let me get this straight," Mr. Shook said. "Kimmie slipped off the boulder and fell into the lake. A life preserver appeared out of *nowhere*. She put it on, and floated in the freezing water until you rescued her."

"Right," Scott said.

"No." Kim crossed her arms in frustration. Other than the bandage on her forehead, she looked fine to Robbie.

"I *told* you. After I fell, I don't remember anything, other than banging my head on a rock. The next thing I knew, Scott was yelling at me and pounding me on the back. I don't know where the life preserver came from. I did *not* put it on."

"Then who did?" Scott scoffed.

Kim grinned but said nothing.

"The *important* thing is that Kimmie is all right." Mr. Shook sat at the table and patted her on the hand. And, Son, I'm proud of you for going to the lake after her. You did the right thing."

"Well," Scott said, pretending to pat her other hand — but it was more like slapping it. "She's a pain most of the time. But she *is* my sister."

He laughed until Kim whacked him on the head.

"Now, about the stuff that was on top of the refrigerator," Mr. Shook began.

"Look." Beka leaned over to show him her locket. "Here it is."

Robbie held out his arm to display his watch.

Thatch joined in, shaking his head and making the chain collar jingle.

Scott pleaded innocent.

"I gave the things . . ." Kim paused. "I put the things back where we found them."

Her father gave her a puzzled stare. "Fine," he said. "I guess that solution is acceptable. I'll call the newspaper and cancel the ad."

He yanked back the kitchen curtain. "Look, kids, the sun is out this morning. Go enjoy the rest of your vacation. And *don't* go to the lake alone."

With the stern look he was giving them, his kids had to agree.

Scott went upstairs. Mr. Shook pulled the phone from his pocket and headed out to the deck. Kim stayed at the table.

"Let's go exercise Thatch," Robbie said, preparing to *smoosh* out the window.

Beka grabbed the dog and got into position.

"I wonder . . ." Kim began.

Beka looked at Robbie. "Is she talking to us?"

"Who else?"

"I wonder if the ghosts really *did* save me." She looked around the room, as if waiting for a sign. "It *had* to be them."

Nothing happened, so Kim rose from the table and carried her breakfast bowl to the sink.

"Oh." Beka reached into her pocket. "I almost forgot." She pulled out the broken bracelet she'd found on top of Zuffel Rock, only it wasn't broken anymore.

"I fixed this last night," she said, setting the bracelet on the counter. When she moved her hand away, the bracelet shimmered, then shot off rainbow-colored sparks.

"Bingo," Robbie said, always amazed at the sight.

Kim rinsed the breakfast dishes, then grabbed

a sponge to wipe the counter. Her gaze landed on the bracelet. Slowly, she picked it up and slipped it onto her wrist. "Wasn't I wearing this last night?" she whispered.

"Nice touch, Raz," Robbie chuckled. "Now let's *smoosh* our way out of here."

Outside, the morning was sunny and warm, with no hint of yesterday's gloom. It was a day that matched Robbie's mood — his mood *after* the *smooshing* headache subsided.

Full of energy, the twins raced Thatch all the way to Juniper.

Thatch won, of course. He always won their races.

Rules to be Ghosts by . . .

1. Ghosts can touch objects, but not people or animals. Our hands go right through them.
2. Ghosts can cause "a disturbance" around people to get their attention. Here are three ways: walk through them; yell and scream a lot; chant a message over and over.
3. Rules of the world don't apply to ghosts.
4. Thatch's ghost-dog powers are stronger than ours. He can do things we can't. Sometimes he even teaches us things we didn't know we could do.
5. Ghosts can't move through closed doors, walls, or windows (but we can *smoosh* through if there is one tiny hole).
6. Ghosts don't need to eat, but they can if they want to.
7. Ghosts can listen in on other people's conversations.
8. Ghosts can move objects by concentrating on them until they move into the other dimension and become invisible. When we let go of the object, it becomes visible again.
9. Ghosts don't need to sleep, but can rest by "floating." If our energy is drained (by too much haunting or *smooshing*) we must re-

turn to Kickingbird Lake to renew our strength.

10. Ghosts can move from one place to another by thinking hard about where we want to be, and wishing it. All three of us must be touching to make it work.

Don't Miss!
The Mystery of One Wish Pond — Ghost Twins #2

Suddenly a scream split the air, followed by a loud crack and a *swooshing* noise. The cousins scrambled from their sleeping bags and fumbled in the dark for their jackets.

Chills raced up Beka's spine. "Good job, Raz. You scared *me* that time."

The cousins stood frozen, panting hard, backed so close against the fire, Beka was afraid their clothes might scorch.

Robbie touched her shoulder.

Flinching, she turned to face him. "How'd you get behind me? I thought you were over there." She flung her arm in the direction of the noise.

Before he could answer, she continued, "I think it's time to stop making spooky noises. I'm starting to feel sorry for these guys."

Robbie's face looked as pale as one of the cousins.

"Rob, what's wrong?" Beka asked.

"I didn't make those noises," he stammered. "I-I thought you did, while I was circling around behind you."

Then Beka noticed Thatch's fur. Standing on end. A growl in his throat erupted into a suspicious howl, unlike anything she'd ever heard.

About the Author

Ms. Regan is from Colorado Springs and graduated from the University of Colorado in Boulder. Presently, she lives in Edmond, Oklahoma, sharing an office with her cat, Poco, seventy-two walruses, and a growing collection of ghosts.